Rush

Of

Many

Waters

Also by Pauly Hart

Novels:
By the Gates of the Garden of Eden
Novellas:
Superior Respondent
Ouesso to Epena
The Book of Lesser Voices
Mountain to Mountain
The Word of Yahweh unto Enoch
Empire of the Dragon
Finance:
The Richest Man In Babylon Continued Stories
Collections:
Sometimes I Write Tiny Stories
Adelphoi
Poetry:
Stupid Mind Tricks
Book of Love and Laughter
The Cross and the Poet
What is Poep?
I Love You More Than a Fox Loves Blueberries
The Night Clerk Held a Broken Pencil
Spontaneous Psalms
Kick the Prick
Exegesis with Co-Authors:
My Flat Earth
Biblical Cosmology, 8+ languages
Translations:
The Testament of Job in Modern English
Children's:
Mathmagician and Other Tales of Awesomeness
Periodicals:
Modern Epistle (1-8)
Microzine (1-5)
Rush of Many Waters (1-20)
With children authors:
Farrell Family Fables
With Co-Author Jennifer Hart:
Adulting: A Daily Guide on Being an Adultier Adult
Audiobooks:
Biblical Cosmology
Superior Respondent

Rush of Many Waters:

Volume Sixteen

By Pauly Hart

Contents

Shorts

After the beanstalk

Jack Spriggans lived in a town called Crep. Crep was a non-specific and boring town in almost everything. It had a modest amount of cows, a decent amount of stone fences, and your average weather. Crep was located in England, in the western tongue, sometimes called Cornwall. The closest neighboring town to the south was Crow's Nest, and then beyond that was Liskeard. Devonshire to the east had just recently been their enemy during the civil wars, but now they were getting along as friends.

The governor of Plymouth, a mister Ralph Weldon, was a parliamentarian. He was a good man, and even though, Crep and its surrounding neighbors were in Cornwall, and he was in Devonshire, he had no problems with their Catholic ways, and left them alone, because he detested war and was quite tired of it. He himself had fought in the first English Civil War and wanted only peace to remain.

Jack Spriggans and the host of tales that surround him are lost to our history books due to the wars and battles that had erupted over all of England, Scotland, and Ireland. In the year of our Lord, 1650, the ending of the second English Civil war had just taken place and the Third English Civil War had just begun.

Life in Crep had gone on in Crep as usual and it didn't matter what the Nobles in Penzance were doing, Mary Albert Spriggans and her only son Jack were paupers and tried daily to make their best of life in their conditions. It didn't matter to them who sat on the throne, or what Parliament had been effected that day. They only worried about themselves.

Crep itself was not even really a town. It was a collection of around eighteen houses and a smith. George Waters, the town mason, had gone off to the first war and had died, but besides his bravado and heroics, the town soon sank into the forest, as sometimes these do. The only exceptional thing to happen in Crep was it had one instance of a happily ever after.

An HEA, as "happily ever afters" are called, are rare and few and are not common whatsoever. On our earth, there have only been 15 actual instances of a Class AAA rating HEA, the most famous of which was Cinderella, of course. But the story in question of Jack? It was a solid "A" rating. Not the best, but certainly the most important thing to ever happen there, aside from George Waters that is.

As you may recall, the story of Jack came about in the mid 1700's, almost 80 years after Jack had long since been in the grave. There is a peculiar reason for this, as his grandchildren were keen to keep the entire thing a secret, but we will not go into that directly. The story has been retold and retold until it has lost all of its original truth and regaled itself in pure sentimentality... But our purpose in this story is not to correct these retellings, but mainly to present the ruin that eventually came of the effects of the return of Jack down the beanstalk.
Let us begin.

First of all, let me quash any immediate concerns the public may have about a fictitious sister, Jill or about some notion of a candlestick, or any mention of jumping whatsoever. These are not about our hero, and it is in the reader's best mind to understand that our story is not some nursery rhyme. It is just that, an actual account of our hero Jack into the real world, having to do real world things, with real world people. This is not a fairy tale per se... Except for the house in the sky and the magical artifacts that Jack returned to the ground, of course.

Cornish history may indeed show a tiny glimpse of our hero, in his right. Recently at the Bodmin Library (west of our hero's now derelict location) I was almost able to obtain historical records of our case, however, the book in question had gone missing. Nonetheless, this accounting is true and factual and if your time prevails, you may find out the facts on your own.

The second issue I would like to discuss is the idea that there was a race of overly large men living in the clouds there above Cornwall and that they made war with the people below and there was a massive battle that ended with the triumph of humanity over the hordes of sky giants. This is, of course, the most ridiculous fable ever imagined. There was not an army;

there was only a small family of Tuath Dé Danann that resided there, for such they were.

The idea that the Tuath Dé Danann were ogres or grotesquely large men, is also a fiction. For indeed, Jack had stumbled upon the great old ones, the Fae Folk, or Fairies as it were, and not trolls, ogres, orcs, or malformed creatures of any kind. While it is true that the Fae exist in tiny proportion than mankind, it is not true that they are in any wise related to the Nephilim Spirits that sometimes stories are told about. However, for the sake of the readers mind, in simplicity, we will stick to the term: "Giant" for ease's sake.

The particular giant family in question was that of Áinfean Daigh. His name (meaning "Violent Fire") is apt enough for lore, but in this case, true. He was an ill-tempered giant who hated most men and loved only him, his family, and others of his kind. His wife Séadhna, and his two sons Domhnall and Uallgarg, along with their daughter Cassán; lived in relative harmony in the Fae world above men.

They were, of course farmers, as most giants were in those days. They had a little plot of land that they worked. They had in their possession a small herd of goats and sheep, three cows, two horses, two dogs, a cat, and five chickens. Here I must take yet another pause and tell you that there was no goose involved. The story of the goose that laid the golden egg was a fable by Aesop and it was written over two thousand years prior. I have no research saying whether the goose was real or fiction, as it is beyond my purview.

Now, it may surprise you that giants were farmers. For if you imagine them to all be gold-smiths or poets, you are living in a fantasy world. Giants (or more specifically: The Fae) were peoples just like you and I in that they ate, and drank and had lives that needed living. Áinfean and his family were the self-sufficient kind of giant who worked a hard day's work and took Saturday off to rest (back then, even the giants observed the Sabbath). They were almost everything that you and I are today... Except that they had no electricity, no automobiles, and they lived in the sky.

And so it happened that one day Jack was working for his mother. Their only cow, Milky White, had stopped giving milk. Jack takes the cow to market, trades it for some beans, his mother gets mad, throws them out the window... Etc... You recall the story. Or do you? Would it be best to recite the events in chronological order so that you may be more well versed in the full history of it all? Mayhap. I think I (for the sake of being pedantic) bring you a small summation of the rest of the events there. Not overly annoyingly so, but a taste, nonetheless.

Ah, where was I?

Yes. The beans go out the window. Jack, alone in his small attic bedroom, falls asleep and wakes up the next morning only to discover that the strange man who had traded the cow for the beans had not been a liar. Jack jumps out of bed, latches onto the beanstalk, and climbs it. It was a long climb. Without having breakfast or lunch packed, he eats some of the beans on the vine. They are delicious and fill him completely.

He reaches the top, steals a bag of gold sitting by a fence and heads home. He meets no one on this first journey. The climb home is exceedingly long and it is well into the next day that he returns. As he comes home, he notices that there are people all about and there is of course, his mother worried sick about him. They steal away inside and Jack discloses his adventure of seeing giant stables, giant tables and the giant chest where he had gotten this gold.

Of course the bag had been filled as he had plundered it, but on the way down, he had dropped one or two or eight pieces and one had killed a pig that Old Man Sparney had raised from a piglet but he was killed with a golden slug, so Old Man Sparney considered this a gift and never complained, and celebrated with several ham dinners soon after. Jack was concerned about the coins and so he and his mother cracked them in smaller pieces (a giant coin was about twice as large as a regular coin) to buy supplies and things for around the house. The other gold pieces were never found. Jack supposed that someone may have found them and hidden them away, but he never learned the truth of the matter.

Now, Jack and his mother were poor even by the standards back then. Yet, here they were with a bag of gold in their possession. Their first inclination was to move to the city, but then, what would become of their beanstalk and the new bean business she had started? His mother hired some workers and made a fence around the stalk, and even their whole property, adding a nice stone gate at the front. She bought cans for the beans, they bought another cow, some guineas (which are like geese, but much more annoying) and a pet dog, whom they named Patience. She was a wonderful dog but sadly does not appear in our story much except at the very end.

But very soon, not knowing how to handle wealth, they were out of gold. It was a very quick and surprising turn of events. His mother, Mary Albert, even had some suitors come calling… Even if they were just there to look at the stalk. None of them would acquiesce to Jacks status in the house as the new bread-winner, and as quick as they had come, they left. Even Old Man Sparney had come calling. He even brought some ham.

A month later, having heard the tale on the wind, the high Sherrif of Cromwall, John Lampen paid a visit. Then his successor, Andrew Trevill had also paid a visit. Both were perplexed, aghast and bedazzled at the overly-large vine that took root in the Spriggan's side yard and reached to the sky. John Lampen dismissed it as a mirage, but there is some mention of it in the chronicles of the office of High Sherriff in Andrew Trevill. The next Sherriff, Richard Lobb also quickly dismissed it as a lark and nothing more came to it from the government… But we are skipping ahead of ourselves.

So!

Soon after the depletion of the bag of gold from the small economy of Crep, there was a lull in the spending habits of all around. Mary Albert no longer needed fence builders or painters or guinea salesman. It was a boom and then a bust. The people who had benefitted from the extra labor were now, again, jobless and went back to their regular lives… Their money that Mary Albert had paid everyone was quickly spent by them on frivolity. The only benefactors in the long run were the Spriggans. They had a new fence and were a little better off, but this would change quickly.

Jack soon decided that he would take another trip up the beanstalk.

5

Now, Jack at this time was twelve years old. It had been a full month since his first climb up the stalk but he was determined to go up again. The leaves on the stalk were still green, and had remained so during the winter much to everyone's surprise. The root base had become a rich golden-green and there were hawks and other birds who had built their nests in the stems and branches. At one point, his mother had thought about hiring some workers to guard the base of the tree, for the neighbors had been seen up it, harvesting (stealing really) some of the overly large beans.

This is a side note in the story that needs to be mentioned. At the time of the first sighting of the beanstalk by Mary Albert the fateful morning of its growing, it had not finished growing. For indeed this is the answer to the mystery as to how Jack was able to rise so rapidly up the stalk to begin with: It had been growing as Jack had been climbing it.
Even as Jack had been climbing the stalk, his mother, back on the ground, had been furtively picking the beans as they sprouted and placing them inside the house. When Jack had arrived home, he had slept outside the first night, for there was no room. The house was been full of beans.

At any rate, during the course of the next little while, she had been busy packing and preserving beans and selling them, even so far away as Perranzabuloe. But within months, there were no more low beans to harvest, and her business went under, even though orders and money still made their way to her doorstep. She was forced to return them and the only fame she created for herself was infamy and poor business practices. Now she sold empty jars.

And so Jack got it into his mind to go up again. This time, he took a newly purchased dagger, a knapsack, some rope, and some food in a small bag. He knew it would be a hard climb but was ready to take the risk for the reward of another bag of gold. On the way he encountered what nature had created for itself. Angry swarms of goldfinches, hordes of pigeons, slews of robins, several families of harriers and one especially angry osprey who dove at him for over an hour.

On his way he saw several good beans. His plan was to cut them off and let them drop to the house below. He did this for the first hour, but after a while, realized that they would only damage the house or kill someone, so he stopped. At night, he slept in the stalk, lashing himself to a good area that served as a sort of hammock, and late in the morning, he reached the clouds.

Now, as I have on purpose failed in the recap to mention anything of the house in the sky, or the surrounding farm around it, I will do so now. It was as you may expect a working giant's farm to look. A high cottage covered in a thatch roof, with wood fencing around. Some of the roof had been decorated in tile. The house was a cobb and log construction while the barn was simply a lean-to of timber. There was a long porch that wrapped around two sides of the house and there were two more out-buildings, also of cut lumber. From Jack's perspective (so low to the ground) everything appeared out of proportion.

The bean-sprout had come up from his sky onto their land just at the southern base of a long wall. Somehow the stalk had grabbed this wall and done its best to sink its tendrils everywhere it could, for security. They could not see it from the house, It fit so nicely with the rest of the shrubs and bushes along the border of the property line so there was no suspicion of anything that could have been awry in the giant's minds, even though, back home, the sprout had been a thing of wonder for over a year.

6

Now, you might think that giant people would also keep giant animals. This is not the case. There are no such things as giant cows or chickens or geese or dogs. If there were, they were all wiped out during the great flood of Noah, along with the dinosaurs, and they do not appear in our story. What is more likely, and indeed true, are that there are regular sized animals who walked and lived and slept and had regular sized lives, in the sky with the giant people. This might seem strange to some, but if one recalls their Bible stories, even Goliath was too big to ride a horse and had to walk everywhere... At least that's how some Bible scholars like to tell it. But Goliath was only nine feet tall. The Daigh family were almost thirty feet tall. Well. That is to say, Áinfean was. His wife Séadhna was around twenty five feet tall, the sons Domhnall and Uallgarg were fifteen feet tall and their daughter, little Cassán was only five feet tall. Cassán was only twelve years old, but in giant years, that made her around the age of six, since giants only age at half the speed as people back then.

Cassán Daigh was out in the fowl coop feeding the chickens, ducks and geese. They had quite a number of all of them, because they needed their eggs every day when Séadhna would make her famous "100 Egg Omelette Surprise". She did this almost every morning, even on the Sabbath. Now, concerning this, I wouldn't want you to be ignorant. Giants of course didn't like God and they thought all of His commandments were silly, so, not only did Séadhna make omelettes on Sabbath, she also killed, processed and cooked them up with chunks of swine. Oh yes. The Daigh family were quite famous for their swine-keeping. All of the giants knew about it.

But enough about Omelettes. As I said only moments ago, Cassán Daigh was out in the fowl coop feeding the chickens, ducks and geese. It was quite a spectacle and it created quite a racket. This, of course, was the first thing that Jack heard when he came to the top of the beanstalk. But what happened next, may surprise you.

End of Part One

Idiot Next Door

Russell Meecham's penis hung out over the top of his men's boxers. It was full of veins and hideous. His pants were wrapped around his knees like a magical talisman. He burped and asked me if he could get me a drink. He had just urinated on the side of my house.

"No, you may not, and I'm calling the police." I informed him.

"Fine. Do whatever you want. But I was going to invite you to Florida with me... Just so you know." He pointed his finger at me with the hand that was still wrapped around the Coors Lite. "But I didn't hit your car!" He yelled as he stumbled into his garage.

Our backyards touched each other, but there was a green-space to the left of my house where I parked my vehicles. He always parked on my lawn and he always bumped my car when he came home. No matter what I tried, he always parked on my lawn, and he always took the turn too wide. The entire side of my silver Toyota Corolla was covered in blue paint from his Buick.

I dialed 9-1-1.

"We're sorry" a voice said, "The number... 9... 1... 1..." a different voice said, "has been changed." The new number is...' IS NOT AVAILABLE'," the different voice said again, "Please consult your directory." said the first voice again.

What the hell? I dialed the operator. At least that number would be the same. It was, but she wasn't having any of my shenanigans and would connect me, but was going to bill this number as a long distance connect. Fine.

"Hello! Police, Fire or Ambulance?" the woman asked.

"Uh..." was all I could say. Russell was urinating off his garage into my yard, in my birdbath. "Police if they get here fast enough, Ambulance if they are going to take too long. Someone is about to get shot." I said, put down the phone and walked around the front of the house. As I was walking, I heard the Dispatcher yelling at me.

"Sir? Sir? Who is getting shot? Sir?" she said into the chair. Russell was, if he didn't get down.

It was a good thing that Brett had borrowed my 12 gauge. All I had was a baseball bat. It was a Louisville Slugger, of course, and I was thinking that if I beat up on his car instead, I won't get into that much trouble. He's trespassing anyway.

Wait. Am I that much of a hillbilly?

I guess today I am.

There it was, right behind the couch as usual. The familiar weight. I don't know if I would go after the car anymore. It might just feel a little better to go after Russell instead. I opened the front door at the exact wrong second. It didn't matter what my neighbor may or may not be doing at that exact moment to my birdbath.

There in the sky, for all the world to see, suspended in seeming holographic wonder was the King of Heaven. He must have been pretty close and I wondered if my face would melt off. He wore these crazy clothes, like a robe or something that was totally bright red, and he was on this huge ass horse that was as white as his hair. He pointed his sword at the ground and then from all over, the birds started coming.

I mean, this guy in the sky didn't look like he was playing. And I almost would have preferred that to the shit that happened next. With all that stuff happening in the Middle East, I kinda knew that the end was near, but I didn't think it would be like an Alfred Hitchcock movie. At least, it was until the seven headed dragon came up out of the ground.

I recalled singing in the choir about the last days a-comin... But this was just bat-shit crazy. I kinda snapped out of it when the car almost hit me. Red corvette went right into my house, not five feet from where I was. *BOOM!* What a way to go, here at the end of the world. It was my other neighbor, Brineta, who had been watching the white-horsed God in her rearview mirror.

"Well dagnabbit Brineta! I just had this re-sided!" I came in to where she had parked in my living room. A long time ago my double-wide had lost its foundation, and so I had it lowered to the ground. It had set that way, even after the property manager had cited me. I didn't care. Let them cite me. I wasn't paying. I was grandfathered in to this property from my actual grandfather, believe it or not. The code didn't apply to me and she knew it.

I guess the only good news was that it sure made it easy not to kill drivers of cars when they crashed into you. Deloris was hysterical. I realized this almost instantly because of the cocaine on her face, and her dash, and her console, and pretty much all over the inside of her car. How much was that? It couldn't have been less than a quarter of a kilo. Dang Deloris, and I thought I had problems.

"God damn it, Steve!" She frantically fought her seat-belt. "Damn it! Damn it! Damn it!"

Who was St... Oh. Steve was probably the dead guy in the backseat. I don't think she knew he was dead. And I was about to tell her when someone in a white horse landed on my roof. My dad cleared his throat, the way that he always did, when he wanted my attention. That was surprising however, as my dad had been one of the abductees back a couple of years ago when *they* came. He was supposed to be dead, yet, here he was, astride a white horse, nonetheless.

"Son, you're going to want to watch this. I'm going to go kick some satanic booty," he said.

He always called it that whenever he was praying or helping out at church. Church! We were always the first ones there and the last to leave and I had hated it. It was weird to hear him say that again after three and a half years. But there he went, galloping off the roof, saving the day.

It was kinda nice to see good old dad again after all that time. Glad to know he had been doing well at the end of time, off to fight another battle. Off to kick some satanic booty. Too bad I wasn't going with him. Yeah, I guess that meant something else for me. "That was alright, wasn't it?" I thought, feeling the old familiar weight of the bat in my hand…

Sure it was.

As long as I got to take out some of my frustration on Russell.

Non-Interaction

As I lay awake in bed
At night I realize just what
this is to be awake
and wanting the incredible
mind numbing mental stimuli
of this screen mentality
called the vision of the telepaths
In this state, I seldom
rest my mind on what my friends
are doing, where my family is
what the affairs of my pocketbook are
or what my place is in this world
I just want to watch T.V.

I have been lured into this
false perception of reality in thinking
I have had the goggles of
madness affixed onto my face
I am afraid of who I am
I must escape, escape, escape
Springer, Seinfeld, Friends and Alf
These false realities are persuasive
But these persuasive realities are false
I lay awake, awake I lay
and toss and turn and think
About laying in my bed awake.

But I so crave this insatiable
spirit crushing mind drug
of my monitor in space
launching into a fantasy realm

where bad is arbitrary
and good is circumstantial
It is in this ashtray that my soul lingers
The conversation killer
The friend of the damned

I have been hooked, lined
sunk and beached
into this slough of despond
And I wither, growing faster and slower
And chuckling all the way
For this life is not my life
So I enjoy it better, but
am not the better for it.
I sink, I sink, I sink

A brave new world, THX 1138
Blade Runner and Fahrenheit 451
Max Headroom and 1984
The Television is the chiller of my core
I take it upon myself to place blame
I take it up-on myself to be shamed
I bring it towards myself. I inflame.
I place it inside myself. A new brain.

I have found this life interesting.
Much more so than my own.
I am quick to recognize nothing.
I am slow to absorb life's transmissions.
When the televisions are so much easier.
I sing their songs, feel their pain.
Believe their lies, purchase their products.
Make good on their warranties and
then watch the re-runs.

This non interactive virtual reality
talks all day long. It is impossible.
It is incredible. It is preposterous.

It is an insane waste of time.
Television pillages the heart.
Television rapes the mind.
I must believe in television
For if I do not and am not like them
Then I am a loser, and there is
something wrong with me.

inexplicable

sex with you
is something special
sex with you
is very nice
i didn't know that
we had problems
until
last night

so i will try
and
comprehend it
i will
come and tackle you
i will drive you
wild with pleasure
and
make you cry

have some faith
and
have some patience
let me warm up
to this life
sex to me is
something new

and i want to
get it right.

kaylee

keep on trying
without dying
make it true
don't delay
try and live
within your head
create in there
a friend: true
skip your fears
face your foes
and always think
you are the best
keep on believing
don't forget
who you are
regret nothing
forget nothing
forgive, forgive, forgive
soon you'll find
just what you need
and life will smell
like fresh cut roses
but it will still
look like thorns

The burn

Shall I never end this burning sensation?
The Lord did signs and wonders for all.

But the all forgot the all he had done.

He opened up his mouth with teachings and parables.

And we shoved our prejudice down his throat.

He trod the second mile for us.

But we tripped him and whipped him and made him bleed. The sensation started at my hands.

I remember when he smiled at me.

And I bashed his face in with my club.

His well trimmed hair and beard.

It was in my hands in bloodied clots.

The anointed one of Israel hung from a thieves gallows.

It was my hands that nailed him there.

That burning, it scorches and gnaws at my arms.

His clothes. . . we stripped him like a whore.

We wore our pride like jewelry, and it blinded him.

We were drunk on power, but we gave him vinegar.

Could he still know? I stabbed him with my spear.

The blood, the water, it stank of forgiveness and love.

Up my shoulders and around my neck the burning crawls. The birds, flies and bugs ate at him like a carcass. The sun and the wind tortured his mind. The rocks that were thrown, bashed at his bones. The yelling, my cursing, my hatred toward him boiled. Still the passionate burning persisted until it consumed me.

It engulfed me like a living fire. For it was I who killed the carpenters son. It was I who killed him. It was I who nailed him up on two planks of wood and left him to rot.

It was I. It was I. It was I.

And the burning still burns.

Change and Escape

Change is violent
Wrapping around
Clinging to me

Disarousing trial

Change comes to
Those unexpecting
Change is wicked
And hurtful and mean

Change to you
Change towards the
Future of our little
Experiment in love

Go ahead and cry
No one has hurt me
As much as you have
Girl, Go cry, Fly away

You said you wouldn't
You lied through teeth
The same that punctured
My ready willing neck

Liar. You are nothing
I am the someone
And I still hold on to me
For I am the loved one

Breath of God

As dawn breaks, the new day
skips over the cloud tops breathing.
"How can you breathe?" I ask the day.
"I breathe because the Lord has first breathed me."

As morning wakes, the meadowlark sings
his morning song of happiness and joy.

"How can you sing?" I ask the lark.
"I sing because the Lord has first sung me."

As the sun rays shine, the morning dew
shines itself upon me.
"How can you shine?" I ask the dew.
"I shine because the Lord has first shone me."

And as night falls, I, already asleep on my bed,
forget the beauty that the Lord gives each day.
"How could I have forgotten?" I ask the Lord.
"You forgot because you first forgot me."

But still on me, the Lord . . .
    Breathes, sings, and shines.

He was Gods child

He had dirty hands, and matted hair.
He was a poor boy who wore clothes with holes.
He slept in a small cardboard box.
And he always sang the blues.

But he was Gods child.

She wore thick glasses and had freckles.
She had pony tails and wore braces.
She was pear shaped with unsightly wrinkles.
She wore orthopedic shoes with a bad aroma.

But she was Gods child.

He had an ugly face and had grubby hands,
He was a poor boy from a large family.
He didn't have many friends, he was misunderstood.
He hung upon a cross, pierced between two ugly thieves.

But He was Gods child.

Yes, He was Gods child.

Gormondel

Late at night, under the stars,
When the moon reaches its zenith.
Gormondel comes, to eat just one,
Then shrinks into the shadows.

The children hide, coyotes cry,
And owls, even find shelter.
For in that time, Gormondel's prime
The earth denies her brother.

On one such night, the nighttime's noon,
Gormondel hunts her dinner.
The slorid slump, the black ooze thump,
She rises into terror.

The thickened air, the putrid breath,
She sniffs and tracks her victim.
Not one per chance, now be it two.
For twins this fate is given.

The day is done, the food's away,
The cottage dry and hidden.
Father and mother and babies rest,
With horse, and ducks and kitten.

A winter's night, the first snowfall,
Fire embers glow and darken.
All snug with dreams, and mother's cream.
The house, in peace, unshaken.

The window fogs from gloomy breath
The eyes look out the window
A long soft hand, pressed up against,
The slinks into the rafters.

A muffled thump, the slowing hearts
Gormondel drinks her fill,
The next day's sun, the dead are done,
The grief will last forever.

Spontaneous poem #4

Just like the worlds seashore
I am washed away
But like the tide
I'll come again someday

I am taken for granted
and trod underfoot
but without my hold
the world would split

I am endless and seamless
I am the beach-line
But without the land
I am no good at all

I am never just wet
or never just dry
I wander and waiver
like a meandering fly

But as I am always
And ever shall be
The water, my past

You are dry land to me

gave it all away

I've had all that there was to have
Waves upon the sand, holding me down
Everything that I wanted…

And all that made me drown
All that consumed me
All there was and everything within

The all-consuming desire
All I was within the moment
The incredible pulse

Of the temporal cosmos
All around me – the creative purge
Becoming nothing was all that there was

The great black engulfing
All that there was and…
I stood there waiting for nothing

Nothing was all that there was
And I am left grinning for the fact
That I have nothing else to give

Back to the all that was…
To the infinite nothing…
To where I was going…

Where did I get off on this… this…

Crazy see-sawed nothing… Alas…
I become divorced from my own playground

I find myself wandering alone
Aghast and aloof from my own self
And my own wanton desires

But I do want something
Fucking insane that's what I am
I am a topless strip-tease bag of shit

Here in this insipid fecal society mine
The desire… desires… insanity
Just relax my soul… just be…

Recant all dissident wanderings
Replace all of the was…
With what will be.

Essays

An essay on the hardship of love

There she was, sprawl legged and lounging on my brown chair in my living room taking up my time with her mischievous eyes... what did she want? Why was she here? And why did I find myself over the next few months falling deeply and more madly in love with her?

Could it have been the way I would see her play with her children? The way that she adjusted, fidgeted with, combed, flipped and plainly USED her hair as a weapon of attraction against men? Perhaps it was her readiness to serve that became the main appraisal point in my estimation of her worth in my life. Most of all, yes, most of all, I believe that we were meant for each other... That there indeed were those rare couples on earth that despite all obstacles and hindrances, actually finds their one true destiny. Their love. Their soul mate.

Yes, there she was. And I fell.

Ok, let me back up for a bit. When I say that I "fell in love" I don't mean that I had been casually strolling down life's lane of bliss and joy, hands in pockets, eyes darting across a perfect sky and ears attuned to the chirp-chirp-chirping of blue jays and whoops there's the proverbial manhole cover left off and down I go! No. Not that at all.

What I mean when I say: "I fell in love" was that I had been Indiana Jones running through the opening sequence of Raiders of the Lost Ark. Booby-traps and deadly pitfalls avoided I now come crashing out of that dank place like a bat out of hell, and find myself alive and unscathed... terribly dusty in the glimmering sunlight... I have escaped it all I think to myself, but it is only then that I notice the forest of punji sticks pointed at me, and the sixty beady eyes of the angry natives.

I fell in love. And it was a whole new set of rules.

Make no mistake dearest reader, I have been in love before. I loved my first woman in college. I loved another shortly thereafter, and, I married her. Yes this is no new subject to me... this whole attraction between man and woman thing. However, up until this time my marks have only been "Satisfactory". It has only been recently that I have found myself wanting to re-enroll in this school of love and try again for better marks.

So here I am, pained and healed, cut but mended, wounded yet remedied, ailed but cured. Back from the dead once again like a Frankenstein's Monster. And like a forlorn infantryman in some World War Two era forgotten post of some odd North African battlefield, I have that same look of horror in my eyes. That do or die syndrome. I see the enemy (or in this care, the subject of desire) and it just mortifies me... no, TERRIFYS ME... that very very very soon, I will most assuredly arrive upon some decision - life or death- that will affect both of our lives forever.

So, I AM in love. No denying that. But what is it about THIS love that makes the OTHER LOVES seem foolish and immature? Why does it seem so refreshing to me to be around her? Why is it that every breath that I take when she is in the room is scented with incense and nectar? I really don't have any idea why. Oh sure, I guess I could take a wild stab and say: "Aha! Here is why I am inebriated with her." or "This is the reason for my heart to act the way it does."; but in reality, who knows? Who can really tell? Not I for one, and I don't know if even she can tell me what is really going on. You know what though? I won't let this hinder me from finding out. I have no idea, but I will sail on into it un hindered.

Yet I will trust God. Wasn't it He who guided me through the strife and hatred of my first loves? Wasn't it he who cured me of my emotional pains? Wasn't it he who cured me of my codependency? He who soothed my wounds and kissed me to life. yes, it was God, and He made me man enough to trust. Man enough to believe, and man enough to be man enough for the woman of my dreams. The woman of my destiny.

Didn't God give me a plan for her in the Bible? Of COURSE HE DID! Well I didn't happen to just read Proverbs 31 the other day. (You know, I had read it only twice before that.) I can honestly say that Solomon or Lemuel, or whoever-the-heck-it-was that wrote that had such a hard time coming up with that little lists of pre-requisites to guide their hunt by, a goodly and God-fearing woman was sure hard to find! Nigh impossible... But with Gods help it was possible for me!

And even now as I see all the attributes from this chapter come into fruition in the woman I have fallen in love with... I do not believe that she sees herself within the context of this beautiful piece of scripture. Doesn't she know how cool she is? Or perhaps she tries so hard and it never seems like enough, that she doesn't see what she does right but only what she does wrong? I wonder if this is a humility thing? Is this view of her own reality slanted to not realize her own greatness? Oh the pain of those long years in service of a spiteful spouse. How it would relieve me if I would be the one to wipe them from her heart. How much has she been through for the sake of a "normal life"? Has she betered? Have the scars made her strong? Was it worth it to begin with?

Perhaps pain is a bit awkward in that regard. Pain makes you do things you would not do otherwise. Pain just makes you more of who you are. Whether you are a wuss or a war-monger, pain reveals it. That is why they say that the wounded warrior on the battlefield is the most dangerous... he has little to lose. He has tasted pain, and found it real. The fear of the unknown is gone and all that is left is the knowledge that he can perform now what he couldn't just moments before.

Pain is strongest in love. Perhaps this is why so many poets write about it. Love stories are only remembered if they end tragically. And if I have become the man that I am today with the activation of pain, then I am a happy man, because if I never had felt pain, I would never have known truth. Without pain, I would have not learned to learn from my loss, and would not have been the person that I am today. I have come back from the pain, and found my true purpose. I would rather have nothing else fulfill my desires but that which fulfills it to the uttermost.

Pain is strong. The hardship of love is full of it. I have been hurt. I have been used, and abused, sold off, written off... My id, ego, soul and heart have been shamefully treated by both God and man... and did I enjoy it? Did I like it?

No... But profit from it? Yes. I have profited well. Profited and grown. Grown tall.

The hardship of love. Definitely something I write about seldomly, but think of quite often. Is love hard? Does it get any easier? Is difficulty in love something normal? Does it get any easier that what it seems like now? Who knows? Not me. All I know is that, my whole life... my entire existence is wrapped up within the Heavenly arms of Christ. He will catch me when I fall. Yes, falling even into the arms of love. He is there. And He is faithful. Faithfull to heal the brokenness in my soul. Faithful to heal the pain and the grief. To restore and to bring me back from Hell into a newness from the hardship of love.

The unpopular cult of truth

On March 26, 1997, the cult known as Heaven's Gate believed that they were going to be picked up by the alien mothership that was trailing the Halle-Bopp Comet. Using the internet, they spread their ideas far and wide, inviting the serious and committed to join them on their quest for ultimate truth. Then as the comet passed, they committed group suicide. Living and dying for their idea of truth.

This is not the first instance of a sub-culture (or in this case a cult) tying their lives to the ideas of the truth. Let's look at the Jones-town Massacre. The Peoples Temple comprised of 913 souls... Many of them were children. They died following one mans idea of truth. Every year hundreds of people die for what they believe is the truth. Buddhist monks ignite themselves on fire for their beliefs. Political prisoners are executed for their beliefs that differ from their country. Even mortal danger can be included here. I had a friend in college who was at Tieneman Square in Beijing during the riots there. His belief in something so strong, that he was willing to risk life and (possibly worse), social isolation led him to participate in activities not in accordance with the plans of Chairman Mao Tse Dung.

The apostles of the Christian faith were all (save one) killed for their beliefs. St. Peter the apostle was made to witness his wife and children executed before his eyes. As he saw his wife crucified before him, he called out to her: "Remember the cross!" And even he, unwilling to find himself worthy to die in the same manner as his Lord did, offered to be crucified upside-down.

Such was Peters belief in the truth. His truth. This great man was born into his culture, was married, had a fine job and a good life. What prompted him to so drastically change his entire viewpoint. What was it that upset his world so much that he (after spending only three years with Jesus Christ) would renounce his old lifestyle and embrace this new one... Even to the point of death?

When the son of man appears will he find faith on the earth? I often wonder about this. Do we as Peter did, so adamantly believe in the Truth that we are willing to attach our lives to it? To face persecution? Ridicule? Martyrdom? In the book of the Revelations of St. John, we see in chapter twelve and verse eleven that "they" meaning "we" overcame by three things. The blood of the lamb, the words of our testimony, and that we laid down our lives. The word "witness" means in the Greek language: Martyr. This translation gives a whole new meaning to the scripture found in the Acts of the Apostles, Chapter one, verse eight... We will be his witnesses in Jerusalem, Judea, Samaria, and to the ends of the earth (emphasis mine).

Where is this truth that I am speaking of? Not in government, not in educational institutions, not in church, but in the hearts of men. To those indoctrinated by the facts about God I may seem cold and blasphemous to group together St. Peter with the likes of Jim Jones. But to those infused with the truths of God, you will see that I am only speaking of the similarities of willpower when involved in your moral code. For most people, acceptance of a particular doctrine is largely attributed to birthplace, family, upbringing, music and the culture around you. This is not to say that they (or even you) cannot rise above these traits and believe in something higher than the beliefs around them. As a point, it is the person who decides what is best for them. Whether to accept and live in this doctrine, or to rise above and take a vantage point above their doctrine, and find a way to confront the issues that so bother them. They are the proverbial square peg in the round hole.

In the book of Galatians, chapter five and verse thirteen, it is stated that we were all called to freedom but not to use our freedom to indulge in the sinful nature… However we should serve one another in love. When we do see ourselves as free, it is then that we are able to break the idioms that so hold us down to our past, and grasp the new and higher path. The path of truth as written in the Word of God.

What is that path? Where can we find our ultimate truth? What brings our true being into that place where we "see" ourselves and break the chains that held us in the past. In the next chapter we will discuss the three steps that you must have to find the truth of God in your life.

Jenn Hart: Spouse Extreme 5000

I can't just say: "Third Wife" and leave it at that, can I? More like the woman of my dreams. Enter Jenn Hart, extraordinaire. The most terrific thing that I have ever been a part of is to be her friend, her completer, her lover, her husband. When a man finds a wife like this, he finds a great thing, he enters into a new life where pains can be healed and wounds can be washed. She was then and is now, my everything and my home. I love this lady more and more every day than I did when I first laid eyes on her in training class at AT&T Mobility. God has been good to me.

Now, we share everything. We are both introverts at heart so sometimes we bump into each other's schedule and hang out for a while. Most of the time we are happy in our own little corner of the house, doing whatever it is we are doing, not talking but knowing that if we needed it, the other person would be there for us at the drop of a hat. I think I drop more hats than she does, but - whatevs. We met and pretty much moved in together within six months and married three months after that. It was a whirlwind engagement and she demanded that we have a wedding. I had only previously just gone before judges to wed my previous two wives. I was ok with having a wedding if she was ok with pre-marital counselling. Both were worth it. We learned a lot from counselling and we had a great time at our wedding. And then we moved in with John Conrad and his new wife. Imagine that.

Things with wives complicate things. As Jenn and I grew closer together, so did John and his wife and concurrently, John and Pauly drifted farther and farther apart. Because of this new paradigm, it became harder to talk with John about "the weird stuff." His wife seemed to be absorbing all of it but Jenn still had some work to do, so we resolved our differences and each moved out into our own newlywed apartments. That was the best solution. Getting our lives together separately in order not to cut the friendship was key. To lose a brother to petty squabbles was a thing I did not want to do.

Soon, all four of us reconciled our new differences and agreed to go in on a secret base in the woods. Yeah. You heard me. We would go to the far reaches of a family owned property, build a cabin, and start our end-time preparations for the end of the world. We had our land picked out, we had purchased around $10,000 in supplies and had begun to frame out our house. We would build it in 10' by 10' by 10' sections and add on to it as the months progressed. It was better than digging a hole in a basement somewhere, admittedly but still a little silly in the long run. But the point was, we were ready to go off grid, raise our own food and learn the truths of God's Word on our own, divorcing ourselves from the world. We eventually quit the project altogether, citing financial differences with each other, a little disgruntled but happier in the long run. Sometimes your best friend can't be your chief time-investment. But it's better to keep a friend and have distance than to smother them and lose them.

Which brings me to the point of my story of meeting Jenn. Whether we lived in the woods away from humanity or not, didn't matter. What mattered was the soul connection that we had with one another. We shared life and that was good. Our faith connected on so many levels that it made things very easy for us to get along with one another. My only issue seemed to be in convincing Jenn on a lot of the information I had gleaned over the years. It didn't matter to her. She had been raised by her Ultra-conservative mother in a Jewish-Christian fashion. She loves great books and the world of fancy. But she didn't dig on my conspiracy stuff. It just didn't matter to her. And that bugged me for a while. "How could it not matter?" I would scream in my head. Why can't she just *see* what I saw? But, hey, everyone has their priorities. Jenn's isn't in the cloud of the inner workings of the ideas that make the head spin. She wanted to read books and enjoy life. And you know what? That's OK. It doesn't matter what you believe on the peripheral does it? Not really when you strive for a happy marriage. We agree on the big stuff. And that's where we found peace.

Still, every now and again I'll drag her into the office. "Hey baby! Check this out!" And she comes in and watches five minutes or so. After five minutes (I have found) she gets really, really bored but she is attentive because she loves me, and I love her too and keep it quick. Her mind is a deep well and I know the info that I throw at her sticks somewhere. But she doesn't do politics or larger world affairs. She's a care-giver by nature and that personality type is more interested in local happenings. I'm a dreamer and she's realistic. It's amazing that we get along as well as we do, but love is action. I put her above any theological stances that I have. Like with John, I would rather gain a friend and lose an argument - so she respects my zany opinions and I let her have her alone time. We can't convince everyone immediately. Some just don't have it in their world-view. Love is patient, love is kind.